BIRDS

by Jane Werner Watson • pictures by Eloise Wilkin

MERRIGOLD PRESS • NEW YORK

© 1958 Merrigold Press, Racine, Wisconsin 53402. All rights reserved. Printed in the U.S.A.
No part of this book may be reproduced or copied in any form without written permission from the
publisher. All trademarks are the property of Merrigold Press. ISBN: 0-307-10945-3
B C D E F G H I J K L M

In this first book, a sense of the joy and wonder of birds is created for every child through Eloise Wilkin's sensitive illustrations and Jane Werner Watson's informative text. The songbirds in the trees, the waders of seashore and river, plovers and pigeons — over twenty-five birds have been simply described and vividly pictured in a way that every child will enjoy.

Canada Geese

Birds can fly.
They fly high.
Some fly miles across the sky.

Purple Martins

In the spring birds build nests. Not to rest in.
They build nests for their eggs, for their young.
Some birds bring twigs and leaves, bits of string.
Some are neat. They build small, tidy nests.

Robins

Day and night mother bird
and father bird watch their eggs.
They keep them safe and warm.

Wood Thrushes

Soon *chip chip* the eggs crack.
And out slip baby birds.

Mockingbirds

They have no feathers. They cannot fly.
But they are hungry. They can eat. Oh my!

Red-winged Blackbirds

What do the babies eat?
Worms and grubs,
beetles and bugs
and tiny insect eggs.

Bluebirds

Scarlet Tanager

They can eat ever so much—
caterpillars, grasshoppers, ants and
flies and such.

Soon the young birds grow feathers.
They have lessons to learn.
They must learn to mind Mother,
and to find their food.

Quail

Some take a turn at learning to swim.

Mallard Ducks

And most birds learn to fly.

Towhees

Gulls

Terns

Gulls and terns can see fish through the waves.
Down they swish.
Up they flash with fish in their beaks.

Sandpipers

Snipes

Long-legged waterbirds walk on the beach.
They wade in the water.
They run among the rocks.
They eat tiny crabs and bugs they can reach.

Many birds like
grain and seeds.

Chickens, Pigeons

They have short, sharp bills
for pecking. They crack seeds open
or swallow foods whole.

Bobolink in autumn

Bobolink eats most as summertime ends.
Then the black and white and yellow of this
happy, singing fellow turns to a dull brown, as
his travel time rolls around.

Summer passes. Weeds and grasses fade.
Fruits disappear.

Cold winds shake the trees and bushes.
Winter time is near.

Something tells the birds to fly southward.
Off in flocks they go.

Larks and warblers, thrushes, thrashers,
gray geese following their leaders—
off they fly with a honk or a cry.

Now the ground all around is cold.
Some birds stay. They may eat
at your feeding tray.

Chickadees

Woodpecker

Nuthatch

Bread and suet and seeds are the food
a bird needs in the cold.
On the snow you may see
a small chickadee hunting seeds.

The spring will bring back
many birds to sing.
They will nest,
raise their broods,
hunt their foods,
sometimes rest.
The right time for each
they know best.

Wood Thrushes